For Dr Sonia Bernard – J.W.
To Arik, Nell and Ted – T.R.

This paperback edition first published in 2020 by Andersen Press Ltd.
First published in Great Britain in 2019 by Andersen Press Ltd.,
20 Vauxhall Bridge Road, London SW1V 2SA.
Text copyright © Jeanne Willis, 2019.
Illustration copyright © Tony Ross, 2019.
The rights of Jeanne Willis and Tony Ross to be identified
as the author and illustrator of this work have
been asserted by them in accordance with the
Copyright, Designs and Patents Act, 1988.
All rights reserved. Printed and bound in Malaysia.
1 3 5 7 9 10 8 6 4 2
British Library Cataloguing in Publication Data available.
ISBN 978 1 78344 878 4

#Goldilocks

A Hashtag Cautionary Tale

JEANNE WILLIS

TONY ROSS

ANDERSEN PRESS

There was a girl
with golden hair
who used her mobile
phone to share
her photos and
her videos;
no harm in that,
you might suppose.

At first, she posted
boring things –
a selfie in her fairy wings –
and looked for likes
that didn't come
(she couldn't count the ones from Mum).

She thought, as she lay wallowing,
"I must increase my following.
But how can I attract a crowd?
I know! I'll make them
Laugh Out Loud."

And so, she shared on Instagram
her baby brother eating jam,

all smothered in it, head to feet,
her friends adored it: #Sweet!

She shared a talking dog called Rover,

Uncle Richard falling over.

Farting ferrets, frisky rabbits...

little kids with silly habits.

Now her posts got lots of likes.
Her ginger kittens riding bikes
got over fifty thousand hits!
Goldilocks was thrilled to bits.

But then her followers got bored
of funny cats and they ignored
her baby brother's latest antic.
Goldilocks felt friendless, frantic!

Fearful she would fall from fame,
she felt that she must UP her game
and look for something far more daring –
something shocking, good for sharing.

Off she skipped, into a wood
in which an empty cottage stood.

And with a cheeky little grin
she took a selfie, breaking in.

She videoed the table laid
with bowls of porridge,
freshly made.
She grabbed the smallest,
ate the lot and posted:
#Piping Hot!

Then, swinging on the tiny chair,
it broke and flung her in the air.
She didn't care: #Fun!

#Fun!

She filmed the damage that she'd done.

"I wonder what's upstairs?" she said,
and bounced from bed to bed to bed.
And then, collapsing in a heap
upon the smallest: #Sleep.

But as she slept, three bears walked in,
"It's her, there's porridge on her chin!"

"She's in my cot!" cried Baby Bear.
"She ate my breakfast, broke my chair."

The bears were such a scary sight
that Goldilocks ran home in fright.
But it was no good hiding there,
for who came knocking? Daddy Bear!

And Daddy Bear was not alone.
A gruff policeman took her phone.

He'd seen her posts
and all the shares
which proved that
she'd upset the bears.

"You must be punished for this crime,"
he said, "and you must spend your time
inside the bears' house, sweeping floors,
mending chairs and doing chores."

All summer long, she went each day.
No time for phones, no time to play.
Yet even when they set her free,
her posts lived on for all to see!

And still it's everyone's belief
that she's a horrid porridge thief
who doesn't have a single friend.

So please...

... think twice before you send!

Read more in this online-safety series by Jeanne Willis and Tony Ross:

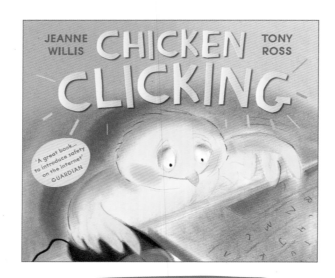

STAYING SAFE

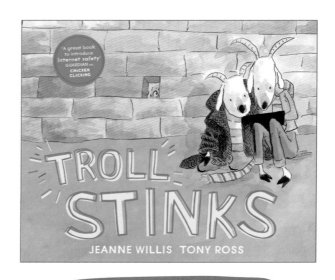

ONLINE BULLYING

For more information and teaching resources,
visit www.andersenpress.co.uk/online-safety